Bonfire Gut Hot

a verse novel

Susan Bradley Smith

Copyright © 2023 Susan Bradley Smith

All rights reserved.

ISBN: 9798390836170

for Mr Brown

I went to the Garden of Love,

And saw what I had never seen.

—William Blake

I am going to fuck up the magazines that made me.

—Kirsty Allison

ACKNOWLEDGEMENTS

This verse novel is a work of historical fiction; no character represents a real person. Historical events and public figures depicted are, however, real, although some artistic liberties have been taken with timelines. Some poems have appeared in other publications: thank you to those editors. The Kirsty Allison quote from the epigraph is used with permission—heartfelt thanks to the writer @kirstyallison_. 'One night in Sarsaparilla: 2050' is devised using a social poetics methodology referencing the cento form, composed from mashup contributions. The misquoted line in 'He Sang, I thought this was love' actually reads '*I thought this was love/but this ain't Casablanca*' and is composed by Chris Bailey from the song 'Casablanca' on *The Saints* album of the same name. The paraphrased quote introducing 'Act 1: Girlhood' actually reads '*I became a criminal when I fell in love. Before that I was a waitress*' and is from the Louise Glück poem 'Siren'. The paraphrased quote introducing 'Act 2: Motherhood' actually reads '…—this/world, in which I've wasted my life/on the ecstasy of craving' concludes the Sharon Olds poem 'That Goddess'. This book is dedicated to Mr Brown, a cherished friend, who adopted our family dog while I was away from home writing and researching in Rome: thank you. Said kelpie also deserves thanks, having overseen the first draft of this book, barking at me each morning during the pandemic when in Melbourne (the longest locked-down city in the world, rumour has it) our household was otherwise asleep and she'd had enough of me at the noisy, antique typewriter: that dog taught me when to stop. To all those whose vintage letters became fictions in this book, friends and family long gone or miraculously still here, thank you for the permission, the inspiration, and the trust—you'll be pleased to know I like bonfires better than archives. Stay punk. Finally, I thank my family, especially my children and husband, for their gracious love and support: it's not always fun having a writer in your midst—you're the best.

CONTENTS

PART 1 | Girlhood: Broken Sonnets

2 | Just call it what it was, the 1970s

3 | Birthday party at Broken Head

4 | Afterparty

6 | Before university became my lover

7 | Sydney is a city full of young and sometimes stupid girls

8 | He sang, I thought this was love

9 | One night in Albion Street

10 | Big decisions after graduation

11 | Flying from Sydney to London

14 | First impressions as clairvoyance

15 | First real party in London

16 | After the IRA bombs, my mother thought I'd die

19 | Boy from the band who fancied life on the Kibbutz

20 | Enclosed

22 | Lisa stayed at home and married a farmer

23 | Chambermaid Sundays

24 | Rare letters, written on prescription pads

26 | Wearing lycra from Pineapple Studios

27 | Young professional late for work

28 | We all came with pasts to our brand new jobs

29 | I did not write home about hesitations

30 | Dressing like a journalist

31 | Letter from a lonesome rock star

32 | You'll be friends for forty berkelium years

33 | That boy, that girl, wanting it all

34 | So many of these people are dead including me

35 | White City Swimming Pool

36 | I'm really worried about El Salvador

37 | Desolation, King's Cross Fire, 18 November 1987

38 | My father does not live off oxygen

39 | Sunday in Oxfordshire

40 | Godless times in Holland

41 | Wedding day ghosts

42 | Other people's parents are nice

43 | Postcards made of tin

44 | To the newlyweds, from a country grandmother

45 | A night out at the Blue Elephant in Fulham

46 | My family is a periodic table

47 | The truth to me is palladium rare

48 | A long letter from my subeditor, or, life under Thatcher

52 | Affluence: amnesia

53 | Everybody has forgotten Berlin

54 | Putney Bridge, Wednesday evening

PART 2 | Womanhood: Prose Poems

56 | You've been married 20 years and watched a lot of TV

59 | You remember East Germany

61 | Keep your linen press in order

63 | One night in Sarsaparilla, walking exempt through hell

67 | The Great Ocean Road, January last

69 | Resignation letter written by wolf-light

72 | Furyology

74 | I still love you (the damage is done)

77 | Rainy day with a merchant banker

79 | After the collapse (pregnant again)

81 | The decisions of women

83 | The niece goes batshit then declares it a draw

85 | You can't really count the ways

86 | Hotel sex before and after it was invented

90 | A short history of thin

93 | Set free

95 | You hack yourself

97 | Glorious micrographica

99 | Today is Friday

100 | One day soon your son will ask if you were ever a groupie

102 | Bonfire night

PART 1
Girlhood | Broken Sonnets

I became a filthy criminal when I fell in love. Before that I was a lousy waitress: as an older woman, considering her youth, our heroine liked to paraphrase her favourite poet Louise Glück.

Just call it what it was, the 1970s

Lots of schoolgirls get lost in carparks after the night is over,
after the stars have done being everclear and started shining
in another hemisphere. They stand alone in these carparks
in the mothering rain, waiting for lifts that never arrive.
The rain is really radium, it rinses them the kind of clean that,
for now, restores poise, fills their empty tanks with courage,
enough to get them home—it's a long, uphill, country walk—
and write sweet notes in their diaries that tell truths which

are also lies about the boy, the music, the kiss, the pub doors
that lured them in like a trapped wolf's smile. The girl plucks
at a wet daisy. *I know he loves me,* she thinks—until the next
day at school and the hopscotch of shame. All the same, she'll
never forget him, even when her teeth are falling out. This is me,
I am that girl. Go ahead, tell me what I did wrong.

Birthday party at Broken Head

It was Christina's 14th birthday party.

I was the new girl in school, shy within the sure-herd of them, bursting with the invite and what it meant. We piled in to her Mum's kombi, I was bashful, fearful, the red-west dirt still in my lungs. *I hope you like your present my mum chose it sorry, sorry.* We drove to the beach, her Mum barbecued sausages and lit the candles on the cake, then left us alone, smoking Benson and Hedges cigarettes, mouth open, eyes closed. So we played, wild and unchaperoned changelings, our breasts were tight bulbs, our roped hair sunray-long, our boom-boom hearts ocean-loud. That day was all gladness. We were dictionary gold back then, while our loose legs still belonged to baby horses, and our hearts to us,

at Christina's 14th birthday party.

Afterparty

1

Amateur theatre shocked my

teenaged, raised-as-Christian soul,

all that kiss-and-slap, the staged

shock of ideas, the adults learning

lines to plays that tore them apart,

from their married lives, their children,

their freshly purchased holiday homes.

I drank the cask wine without being

scolded, and became the girl who

recited a poem about riots in Soweto,

as though I knew. At the wrap party

I kissed the leading lady's son on his

mother's waterbed, potassium

leaking from us in a slow steam.

2

Lonely, afterwards, I hunted

down and found my best friend

poolside, playing his guitar

in the squid of dark, shot by stars.

There was arsenic in the air, also

frangipani. It was the end of

our childhood, but the night

had another understory—we

watched his parents' final fight

about faithlessness by the

brash bougainvillea, his

mother soon to sadly suicide.

Yes, his mother was soon dead,

but we watched her fight.

Before university became my lover

Until then I'd thought them benign but when

my parents said 'University? What for!' and

instead brokered me into a fancy job in men-

swear at our country Kmart the real mystery

is why I stayed, why I moved in with an

electrical apprentice who tried to Catholic

me into marrying him, although luckily

I was still mad from my boyfriend's car-crash

death otherwise I would have forfeited myself

to homemaking instead of partying, instead

of dancing and making the most of our wild,

country-bred, foolish bodies. The ocean was

always close by, fathomless but faithful. Finally,

I followed its pacific, plutonic throb to Sydney.

Sydney is a city full of young and sometimes stupid girls

I got a part-time job there in retail, selling clothes

to happy women. Once, my manageress took

me to her northern beaches home for the weekend,

to surf Box Head with its rare but epic left point—

I thought I'd die, so stayed in bed.

She was a good, clean, chromium kind of friend,

unlike most other people I was slowly getting

to know including the footballers and their wives

who thought it was cute that I went to university—

I did go to university, I was studying law, I think

—but got confused when I missed my boyfriend's

games to finish essays. The music scene was just

as dumb but lots more fun with its hammering harm,

so much energy someone needed to die. It's true.

PS: I married the drummer: my self-esteem was asparagus.

He sang, I thought this was love

the morning after

I had nothing to say about my life that wasn't already in a song, the width of my stupidity astonishes me now but when I went home with the lead guitarist, who was really a tractor, on the night of my engagement party I was sure I'd soon be his for good. I thought, this is love, this is Casablanca. The record on the record player, who was really a taxi, disagreed.

the morning after is always the morning

I'm not sure anyone really thought the 'Tour of Us' would ever end. We recorded a new concept album each night, spun it for the god of neon, who was really police car, watching us kiss and dance and fall with joy. Freedom, though, was really a push bike, and not truly ours to pedal, not us girls: unlike our gay friends, we were just sluts.

the morning after is always, always the morning after

One night in Albion Street

Mostly what I remember about heroin is the waiting,

the slow anticipating, the tender silence that settled

in the room, slant and close, watching a friend

shoot up before the night could commence.

Always, this waiting for something better to begin,

waiting for the flush, the instruments, the deal,

the people. I remember the neatness of the rooms,

their lies of peace, I remember the punch of

the paramedics arrival, them carrying dear,

dead him from our home. The things we did

next, as though lithium had not already been

invented for days like these, I do not remember.

My diary, who does, says *So many gone already,*

their leftover lives gifted to unskilled me to live.

Big decisions after graduation

I drank at the Sydney Trade Union Club

before, during, and after it was famous.

One special night I slept in the cloakroom,

I'd been celebrating, clearly method-acting

my last exam on Russian Romanov heroines,

a History graduate now. What else could I do

but drink myself dead? Could I possibly escape,

or did I now have to work at a bank, or become

a school teacher, as though my third-grade

dreams had arisen to strangle me afresh, or

should I perhaps grow silicon or lavender or

raise lambs? My name was not Mary. I bought a

one-way ticket to London because the world had

rules: you couldn't fly to New York without a return.

Flying from Sydney to London

1

It wasn't really a champagne event,

though it did feel like a wedding, what

with all the family there farewelling me

and marvelling at my misguided departure

outfit (white cowboy boots; Bronte-blue

eye shadow) and my anxiety to get my

sorry soul out of Sydney and her cruel

canopy of sunshine, her oystered,

throbbing nights, her groaning harbour,

her memories sliding down my throat

gagging me with love. I was rich from

waitressing, soon to spend my silver

on the future, never to return, I said,

my heart an unsaddled horse.

2

Changing planes in Hong Kong, a

Security guard pointed a machine gun

at my chest. I wasn't completely asinine,

I had expected difference, but this was

tourism like a ruptured condom, and I felt

once more the pickaxe panic of the AIDS

epidemic. Also, at the same time, that hot,

uranium happiness of things being beyond

my control. University had ringbarked

me. Sure, it had been revolutionary in a

jet-lagged way, but nothing like the rip

of music or men. Please don't kill me now,

I begged, I haven't even learnt to spell

praseodymium, or made it to London.

3

Absolutely nothing matters, not even that

he failed to turn up as promised at arrivals

to meet me and escort me to my new home,

which is his home, shared with his and my

high school girlfriend, in Shepherds Bush.

Instead I stood there alone and over-dressed

like some royal troublemaker on acid in exile,

then moved on to manage the acrobatic feat

of migration, then the luggage, (full of cans of

Melbourne Bitter beer and band t-shirts), then

the opera of the underground—*oxygen,*

oxygen, please give me oxygen—all by myself.

I stumbled forward, madly combusting, into

the interstellar shape of the newly begun.

First impressions as clairvoyance

You will always be—

for some strange reason I arrived at Gatwick not Heathrow. Then, airports were young, they had the personality of what they were built from, and when I landed on its single runway, Gatwick's control tower was still in nappies. Oh Gatwick, how I love you, with your beehive terminal and your little children on family days out atop your tin observation deck, your firstness with a direct link to the city, your Sussexness, the Christmas-present-sized parcels of green kissing your edges, your customs officers who laugh and tease me about winters, who smile and stamp and welcome, because I am from the Commonwealth, because I am white. One day Gatwick you will turn into Heathrow, another shopping mall, but you will always be my helium first,

you will always, always be.

First real party in London

It was Saturday night in Notting Hill before Notting Hill
was Notting Hill. Out of a black cab, in from a dewy street
alive with rain, up a narrow staircase with a spongy tread,
then onto the unsafe rooftop through a room exploding
with boom. The party was another planet, a science fiction
of oxygen. Friends from work lived here rent-free, squatting,
said it was 'power-to-the-people' but really they were just
rich Sydney kids messing with reggae economics. They'd
dash off to Paris with their spare cash when the toilet got
blocked, or it was too cold to sleep without heating. I had
a guitar with me like some shy hippie in need of love, like a
nice girl who wouldn't slept in the bath with her own mercy.
The next morning the man I'd danced with all night smiled
across the bed at me, gallium girl, released into the wild.

After the IRA bombs, my mother thought I'd die

1

There are seven dead horses on the ground

in a constellation of terror, dark stars now.

The soldiers of Elizabeth's Household Cavalry

heading up South Carriage Drive through Hyde Park

became likewise heaven-bound, trapped forever

by boyhood desires *they're changing guard*

at Buckingham Palace all because the IRA had

remotely triggered 25 pounds of gelignite and

30 pounds of nails hidden in the boot of a

Morris Marina. The soldiers of the Blues and Royals

regiment were not saved by love or sovereignty,

in fact it was their duty to this that killed them.

The horses, in their animal way, like my mother,

in her tungsten way, had forsaken all allegiance.

2

A few hours later, the second terrorist attack.

The IRA were questioning the Queen's dominion

and who knew what the military bandsmen

of the Royal Green Jackets truly believed as

they busily, jollily performed tunes from *Oliver*

in a lunchtime concert in the bandstand—until

the bomb, designed to protect bystanders, killed

eight musicians and turned instruments to scrap:

'The Irish people have sovereign and national rights

which no occupational force can put down' said the IRA,

and Prime Minister Thatcher said 'callous' and 'cowardly'

and 'evil' and 'brutal' tilting towards a hot revenge.

Of that sunny, kryptonic day in Regents Park, with body

parts acrobatics of the air, my mother lost all adjectives.

3

Later, Invoking Article 51 of the United Nations Statute,

the Prime Minister got on with her job and declared war

on the Falklands, to secure the right to self-determination

of certain people. It was a wonderful distraction. Elsewhere,

the bomb-surviving, severely wounded guard called Peterson

became a British Military madman. After blaming the IRA for

his post-traumatic stress, the failure of his marriage, and the stabbing of his two children (Ben, seven, and Freya, six), he then knifed himself through the heart. Suicide. His wife Erica had apparently said the wrong thing at a military reunion. Sulfuric nights. Meanwhile, the name of the surviving horse was Sefton, and Sefton became a British national hero. Sefton appeared on many television shows, so my mother told me. She is a great fan of the television, and the Queen.

Boy from the band who fancied life on the Kibbutz

'Dear Suzy of 5/85 St Stephen's Road Shepherd's Bush

London W12: just a quick note to let you know

I've made it back from Amsterdamage with

a few brain cells left, excuse appalling handwriting,

shaky right hand. Great time had but the body

could take no more. Could you either drop me

a line (Flat 5, 70 North End Road Kensington W14)

or call round so we could have a chat sometime?'

He sent me lots of love and a kiss on expensive,

blue, Queen's Velvet Hallmark stationery. In those

days I couldn't see straight, I wore no reading

glasses, the morning post always warped my vision.

I was promised to another but my heart was tin and

lonely, so I went, because stamps are forever stamps.

Enclosed

1 Single Mother (Widowed)

'Your life sounds so full and exciting,

seeing so much of this wonderful world.

We've been plonking on. I've tried in vain

to contact your father, tonight I'll try the pub.

The kids and I are taking a road trip to Brisbane

for Expo 88, visiting heaps of friends on the way—

an emotional contrast to the trip I've been of late!

How could you tell from thousands of miles away

that there was someone in my bed? I went out with

with another guy and Nathan went nearly insane!

News: I've bought some land in the bush; the boys

are mad about football; and my girl is a netballer!'

All this news, five zirconium-thick pages of it, made

me forget Stonehenge, and my reasons for leaving.

2 Fatherless Daughter

'Dear Suzy—Hi! We're all fine. I miss you heaps.

How is your job? Are you going to Scotland

for the winter like you said? Simon and Julie have just been down, they left yesterday. Today George is coming down. The photo of me is in case you get homesick. Guess what?! I've got a duck and his name is Wally Duck! I haven't got a middle name yet, any ideas? Please tell me, have you met any nice guys? See if you can bring one home with you! We've decided to have a surprise party for Mum's birthday. I wish you were here. Do they get *Neighbours* over there?' Now we have a duck in the family, a few doctors, and a future Prime Minister, us girls can relax.

PS Wally Rutherfordium, the duck that drowned, RIP.

Lisa stayed at home and married a farmer

'Sorry for not putting pen to paper before this, time is of the essence these days. Marlow is six-months old already, Astrid is at preschool! It's a wet, subtropical afternoon, feels like flood rain. Your Mum phoned and told Bill you were getting married! You told me before you left for England not to be surprised, but I am. One thing you'll find hard to cope with when you come home is that I don't celebrate birthdays or Christmas or Easter anymore. I'll chat soon on the phone with you about me becoming a Jehovah's Witness.' New, really-giggly her said, 'You should turn on to creation!' So: still a radon bitch.

You can be so much in your life—a dancer, a mother, an adulteress—but never religiously nineteen again.

Chambermaid Sundays

My will is tangled up with helplessness.

Billy has gone out already

to chambermaid her day away,

trading life for twenty-five pounds cash,

which she saves in a private account

for holidays they can't otherwise afford

from her weekday wages because

Gerry doesn't really have a job. I'm not sure

what he does at Trojan Records, but he

took me there once, to the cellar, where

the neatly stacked shelves of vinyl broke

my silly heart with their calcium crunch.

I should go do something to write home about,

but me and my still-stupid heart are idle.

Rare letters, written on prescription pads

1   Prescription: summer holiday

'Hey it's me again how are you going?

You look great from the photos you sent.

Me, well, my hair is bleached from the sun and salt,

my mind is in a good, hippy, neutral-karma state.

Well, almost. I'm filling my (holi)days surfing mals

with Mick at Flat Rock or Wategos until lunchtime,

we come home and make a real big thick sandwich,

then it's too hot to do anything until about 5pm

so I sit inside and watch videos and sleep. Come

the night I walk the suburban streets with mother,

or along the beach, sometimes the river. It's hot.'

Then he drank, and listened to her records by himself,

being alone being a very freaky experience for him.

2   Prescription: Gossip

'Enough of that hippy shit, hippies suck, let's face it,

they don't even immunise their children. If everyone

was a hippy I'd be out of a job. In hard rocking news

The Strap Ons have broken up, but *The Sunnyboys* have reformed, saw them at the Ballina RSL. They played a lot of new stuff which I liked most, one song sounded like *The Stems* (they've broken up). I saw Anthony, he's bought some land at the Channon, he's still with Nola, he must be made of titanium. Sue is here too, you made a fool of yourself at her 21st, remember that? We are doing Accident and Emergency together at Lismore Base Hospital. All of my friends are going to England for their final elective.' He said he wasn't going to use up all the white space just because it was there, and this became his motto for life.

Wearing lycra from Pineapple Studios

This morning South Kensington is a skeleton aching with
Autumn. I was sharing a flat with a Canadian girl who had
a Bachelor Degree in Sailing, and some Australian surfers
who drove through the night to Cornwall to find some waves
one desperate weekend and just never returned to this strange
place, to this tall, balconied, pale-bricked building, windowed
mistress of foreigners without rental references who sell
their dignity in shared bathrooms (one per three floors, with
toilets that belong in a filthy French film). To escape this
pinching squalor each morning I run two blocks north to Hyde
Park, to its regal embrace. I become the seasons, I become
the strict but loving sky, the flooding leaves, the naked wood.

Oh, cold, leaden London, I love you. I hold you lycra-tight,
I run and run through you, master of my own apprenticeship.

Young professional late for work

You snowed on me Abingdon Road, you snowed all over

me one December twilight-struck afternoon at 3pm, on

a day that had begun (I was so young) with wet hair, soon

snap-frozen. In the Shepherd's Bush rush hour on my

way to the tube, late from the Primitives concert at the

ICA the night before, hastily gobbling a banana, a

few men on scaffolding above—soldiers of the harbingers

of gentrification—lewded all over me: *Oi you can suck me any*

any time you like Blondie, don't waste your talents on that!

I blushed and sped up aided by my new Reeboks which had

the English flag insignia on them, my jeans were stone-

washed, plus I had other pedigrees: an education; a job.

Also, a platinum engagement ring, which most women

would kill for. This, I kept it at home in my toiletry bag.

We all came with pasts to our brand new jobs

I was a happy girl from a small town who drank a lot,

had survived a family made of bismuth and growing

up in Lismore, a town named unoriginally after some

place in Scotland. Also needing consideration:

the secret map of the Bundjalung and the red line

of trauma from all our white, saintly, ruinous wars

(thank you, bad ancestors). All these things were

ghosts within me from dawn to dusk, inside my body

which was too young for a synthesizing gaze. At work,

I let my new friends in the publishing house with their

potpourris of debutante delight twine me to them, though

soon one of us will forget joy, and kill herself in Bangkok.

Before those ends, we had precious, happy days, young

women aglow in our very own, magic-stuck fairytales.

I did not write home about hesitations

Playing pool with my German fiancée

against local Brompton skinheads, I lost

my footing. The Atlas pub was quiet inside

from the soft outside-rain, but my mouth was

round and loud with injury, larger by far than

any pool ball, or common sense. I thought the

war was over? That evening was probably the

end of my marriage though we'd not yet even

swapped rings. We finished the game and left

alive, but injured. How very beautiful London

Town was that night, glossy and twinkly on

our close walk home, us children of enemies.

Youth did not gift me much, but I'll never hold

hands like that, shot through with francium, again.

Dressing like a journalist

This lifelong attraction to dead people's clothes,

this imitation game of thrifty glee, means I have the

correct wardrobe to play the Good Girl, nine-to-five it

with glamour, but truly, all disguises are damaging,

they're a passport to nowhere I greatly want to go but it

will take decades more for me to figure this out. I read

my brother's letter from home on the tube to work,

recall that backstage-life and hate the sister-animal

he is missing—I will hate her well into the next century.

Meanwhile here in London the pubs shut at three, this

is how we know to button our smart coats, return to the

office, and finish writing copy, seeking proof of everything.

Until now I did not believe in yesterday's news, or how it

stains and presses upon the caesium pages of tomorrow.

Letter from a lonesome rock star

This is what he said—

'As you know it's summer here. I'm in the kitchen at Smith Street, I'm not sweating because I'm writing to you ha ha. New Year was a typical acidic haze for me, a friend from Melbourne made me try laughing gas—it works well, intensifies the experience. We ended up going to the club, it was fun to be so fucked-up seeing all those familiar faces. I still hate most of them. If you're thinking about coming back to Sydney forget it, the music scene is really dead and so are all the people. All I do is walk around and scowl and be a badass—looks like I'm going to be single for a long time! You know I still feel guilty about London. I'm sorry, but I had a lot of fun thanks to you. But please don't come back—'
He said that. He, whose music had been my motorway, my nitrogen, my noble gas.
—but one day I just did.

You'll be friends for forty berkelium years

There were five girls and three bedrooms in our

West Brompton, top-floor flat: an engineer; an Irish

Harpist; a podiatrist; a diplomat; and me, all in our

first jobs out of university. Fiona built the chunnel,

Siobhan played in the London Symphony Orchestra,

Eva was I think really a trainee spy, and Josephine liked

Iron Maiden more than fixing feet. When the lease was up,

our beginnings now museum pieces, I got married but forgot

nothing which remains my problem to this day. 'This is to let

you know I've arrived and survived Cairo, so get writing,

you owe me a letter, no excuses'. When she came home we

all met for years afterwards, eating giant pancakes in Chelsea.

This photograph, old as petrified wood, proves our improved

tastes in fashion, but not friends, which needed no upgrade.

That boy, that girl, wanting it all

Very tight denim jeans, black silky tops, young bodies,

heels that will kill you with deliberation, cheap gold chains:

that was us girls on Friday nights, furiously alive in Fulham.

The boys were usually too nice for us, what an atomic waste,

we were prowling through the wrong decade. Then I saw him

and his mates, who were shortly willing to pay us to marry them

for an Australian passport. Next thing you know I was meeting

his mother on the council estate, her 2am-face a pantomime

of hope, her locked-safe dressing gown a moral memory. Soon

he took me to an even starker scene upstairs where I did 'Sydney

Garage' and he tried 'Grecian Summer', then some pillow talk:

What do you want? Me, I want it all? I whispered, *I want it all too.*

I left before he woke. I got sad when he never returned my calls,

but he didn't deserve my thin-waisted dreams: I got over it.

So many of these people are dead including me

'It was lovely to hear your voice on Monday morning honey

although I couldn't help but wonder if anything was wrong

then in the afternoon's mail I received a letter from Aunty Anne

asking me to take over your Mastercard payments

as she no longer could. The account is over the limit,

the situation is far beyond me taking care of it.

As you know I haven't a job yet.

Darling I love you so much,

but you have to be responsible for your own affairs.

You've put me through so much angry and hurtful emotions,

but I soon got over it when I realised I couldn't

do anything to help you without causing me hardship.'

Hardship is as hardship does as my mother well knows,

having killed my cat and loaned me out to her brothers.

White City Swimming Pool

Living in Hackney the decade my girlhood died,

I learned my place as a white girl in a Black city,

ceasing the nonsense of petticoats and perfume,

and the unholy antics of bourgeois bitchface.

Maybe life's acumen arrives too early, when you're

still fully foolish with youth, but—my learning had

begun in outback towns where the bitumen ran

to gravel and the love was thin. And now here I am,

working as a lifeguard in White City Pool, perpetually

hungover, periodically saving lives, wondering about

the nights ahead. *Save Me* they'd cry, the kids who'd

never seen an ocean, a beach—even the Thames.

When the wave machine turned on it was true

pandemonium: we all have failures of firmament.

I'm really worried about El Salvador

'Special love to you both as you approach your nuptials,'

wrote my favourite aunty, whose life seemed

to be in a bit of a low-tide mess,

her new boyfriend being her dead husband's doctor

and all: 'Nathan has been very depressed

and I've had to be very understanding'.

Poor her, poor him, but they'll have forty more years

of massively bluffing their way through life together.

Imagine instead they'd both gone to El Salvador,

him a medicine man, her a praying teacher, and

met some war-faring guerillas on purpose, and their

purpose had been lost to goodly revolution?

But it was less than that, just decades of children and

work and sailing, all for nothing that did not anyway end.

Desolation, King's Cross Fire, 18 November 1987

You could smoke cigarettes everywhere, and we did.

A still-lit match landed on a wooden escalator

serving the Piccadilly line found purchase,

then flashed its lewd, prolonged tongue of fire

around like a snake. Our friend was killed on his

way to work. Thirty more were torched, hundreds,

injured, but gossiping in the darkroom all we thought

was, *What an utter bludger he's running late again*,

expecting him to soon blow in in his battered leather

jacket, lipstick on his cheek, jokes on his lips. Yesterday

lies beneath us like a nuclear submarine, our tomorrows

remain full of sirens and smoke. Yet hope pierces through,

punctures our carbon of disbelief. His lost life lurks, a

feasting, sharky shadow, lest we forget to seize, and seize.

For him, we ride escalators of aluminum to the very top.

My father does not live off oxygen

'Hi there how's it going?

Got your letter, it was great to hear from you,

missing you, but I trust all is well.

I haven't had a chance to write sooner

because as you can see we had to move.

Our new unit is OK, clean and bright,

the rent is $20 more per week so that's less beer for me!

Work is very busy, I am now Patrol Commander.

Are you seeing much? You are probably in Greece

in the middle of that heatwave.

Tim Doyle got the letter you wrote to the staff

at the restaurant but his dog chewed it up.'

My father ran out of paper and sent me all his love,

sent me all his love too late, but he thought of me.

Sunday in Oxfordshire

My friend John is made of beryllium, he is strong and divalent and has a car and a girlfriend and is kind. He pities me and my debauchery so champions us to a day in the country that involves hills and impromptu picnics in meadows with good cows. He sings along to the radio, it's Italian opera, and I think to myself: I know nothing of gentleness. When we get to Oxford I want to begin my life again, get it rich, get it clean, get it smart and happy. After the pub by the river we go punting, it was his old life, and downstream, get lost in velvet time. I imagine someone waiting for me at home, someone who loves me, and that their day has also been glad. Friendship strangely arrived is a gift, a stiff nuclear spin for good.

Godless times in Holland

I pursued you through fields of tulips,

my letters answering yours, which

told me in code of your unavailability.

Yet—one afternoon we meet again

in the helium heart of Amsterdam.

I'd flown from London, you'd driven

from Pforzheim, we tried to make

it feel casual, as though we'd never

kissed, or made green promises long

ago in pacific Sydney. Soon afterwards

we married, which is the same kind of

accident as trying to believe in god.

I am mad and hold on to this romance,

I hold on to you with absurd unreason.

Wedding day ghosts

Marbles in the bath with ice and French champagne,

a bridal-linen sheet for our tablecloth, a short man

at my door saying *Sorry* with voltage-yellow daisies,

my black velvet dress and purple suede pumps,

my husband's honest biker jacket, this is it:

the journalist and the motorcycle courier are

getting married, south of the river, north of hope.

The third time we meet we will marry, Jesus-him

had said to me, flooding my colorless xenon heart.

But inside my head is fear, Scottish fortitude, the

blessings of telegrams from home, and determination—

afterwards the ceremony is incredulous to us.

In our elegant riverside mansion we hosted

an unforgettable party, and I rowed and rowed.

Other people's parents are nice

'Just a line to say congratulations,

and thanks for the photos.

We have regular letters from Paulie

but can't communicate with him,

he seems to be having a good time,

though he is sleeping rough

in caves and deserted mansions,

which I'd probably rather not hear about.

But we're glad he's enjoying it all.

Baby Ben is coming along nicely,

walking at 10 months, dear little soul.

We got flooded again last month,

shocking that it happened again so soon.'

Paulie was last seen heading for Portugal,

and (rock on) remains a holy terror of joy.

Postcards made of tin

'Very sorry not to write—slack—please forgive, truck trip

has been great but London to Kathmandu is too much.

We were doing well with our money until Kashmir

and its beautiful array of wonderful things to buy.

We stayed on a houseboat (pictured) on Nagin Lake,

absolute luxury after months of camping.

This postcard doesn't say much.

I just wanted to let you know

we haven't forgotten you.

If you want to write back,

write to Post Restante GPO Chiang Mai Thailand,

we'll be there for Christmas. Hope life is cool.'

They sent lots of love from Jaipur, too casually I fear,

because after all what they had did not last.

To the newlyweds, from a country grandmother

'Many thanks for the nice snaps you sent us,

you all look so happy. Save your nickel, now

you're married! We had eighty wet points

of rain yesterday, but the golf day is still on.

The footy is here in town this Saturday.

Your Mum and brother will be driving down,

we are looking forward to having them both.

'Himself' is still in Sydney as far as we know.

Old dog Nugget is still as fat as ever, little budgie

is as chirpie as ever, especially when I write letters.

I'm still collecting stamps especially overseas ones,

will you save me a few please dears?'

Don't worry darling one, I will kill your ghosts, kill my

sons, for you: be happy, be free—she never wrote this.

A night out at the Blue Elephant in Fulham

Thai proverb: in a town where people wink,

you must also wink. Dad gave us some money:

Take yourselves out for dinner, so we went and,

spent his gold, leaving drunken him at home

with his empty scotch bottles behind our sofa,

their lost-at-sea chiming, desperate, all night long.

Freshly married, unskilled at adult failure, we

ate our way through the thick, spicy situation

in the crowded establishment, too posh for us,

comparing it to Sydney's best, caring little,

because this was home now. This was it, our lot,

these monstrous days of work, the terrible futures.

And yes: retired parents with their cargoes of ruined

desire, hungry for what they imagined we had.

My family is a periodic table

'Can you send a photo from your wedding day in Putney? I wish we'd been there. On Monday we get the keys to our new home and then we will move from one part of Olympiaplatz to another, and in one week, for the first time in my life, I will no longer be a student. Lots of love from your sister.' She was a Prussian pear, she terrified me, we had not invited her or any family to our wedding, but our friends had driven on autobahns, crossed snowfucked France, boarded ferries for England, arrived in London like glamrock panzer tanks.

We got together, praising love, we who knew nothing of the sulfuric, Germanic future to come.

The truth to me is palladium rare

My friend's wife had a baby a few years before I left Sydney,
there is a bewitching photo of me with her on their farm.
How this became the worse lie of my life still shames me—
She's mine, I said at work as it fell from my diary, and
suddenly I was enigmatic, the woman who'd left her child
in mysterious circumstances across the seas. Later,
I had to write to Adeline from Germany, make amends:
*I'm sorry, I think it was about my abortion, please don't
hate me,* and she surprisingly did not, although next century
she did fail to show up in Edinburgh as my bridesmaid—
worse things can happen in a friendship. 'How's marriage? Any
babies on the way? Started the novel yet? London misses you.'

In Pforzheim the post was the only thing that was all mine:
I lived with my mother-in-law, her harpsichord, and son.

A long letter from my subeditor, or, life under Thatcher

1

'Well, as I write I'm still unemployed, but I've lined up
an interview with *Woman & Home* as Deputy Chief Sub,
it's the worst type of conservative mag. I've signed on
for the dole, what a stigma, I felt really unclean when
I got out of the dole office. Had lunch with the editor
of *What's On* yesterday, a real pisspot, we got through
three bottles of Frascati and a vegetarian quiche,
by the end of it all he offered me was freelance work!
I think he was only interested in our publisher's demise,
gossiping like a woman, either way, it put me off drinking
for a while. I was useless all afternoon and wandered
the streets in an alcoholic state. I'm a bit ashamed.'
We all miss the good old days, we all say that, but
sometimes they were as sad as a Coventry Monday.

2

'I still miss the old days and I'm making a concerted
effort not to lose touch. Saw Katie on the bus the

other day, she's still going out with that virile hunk of macho malevolence. Jemma's birthday bash ended in uproar, we had a confrontation with the manager of the restaurant over an excessive bill. We walked out without paying the whole amount, then the cops pulled up with the manager in the back of a black maria and proceeded to take down our particulars. Apparently a civil court case will be pending if the restaurant wants to quibble about a 100 quid. Apart from that it was a great night though Jem hoped it would be better.'

A mild night considering one evening we'd hijacked a big, red bus after a concert at Hammersmith Odeon.

3

'My beautiful, darling Jemma is well and sends a big, big hello. She recently moved up to Golders Green (mega Jewish territory) and loves her spacious attic room. On the work front she's still applying for jobs, temping in the meanwhile for a hotshot design company—just secretarial stuff to stave off poverty for a while. Her Dad leaves London today, heading back to Perth.

Fuck, he went through so much money it was incredible! Lavished gifts on Jem, took her out to plays, restaurants, he even shelled out for a tele and a fridge. Jemma says it's his way of showing he cares, and he's rich anyway. I did feel a tinge of jealousy I can't offer her a swish lifestyle.' He worried if it was a weakness to love someone so much, but they soon had a baby and things improved materially.

4

'Suze I hope your sense of isolation in Pforzheim isn't too Unbearable? Sounds idyllic to me, a typewriter by day, beer and cigarettes and friends by night, so chin up! I did give thought to moving back to Melbourne, but that's all it was, idle speculation. I'm sure I'd be bored shitless in a short time. No, it's better to struggle along in London and hope that someone, somewhere, recognizes my ability. I hope that you're happy. It was a huge upheaval, you can't expect it to be without its traumas. I'm not sure we'll manage to cross the channel to see you. Write to me, or Jem if you have private woman-stuff to discuss: not that anything can shock me after working amongst all you rampaging girls!'

I did not know he would write me such long, precious

Letters; I guess you never miss people until you leave.

Affluence: amnesia

It began outside on the lip of our back garden, which

bled into the Thames like bromine, the annual university

boat race. So pretty. Through our oak front door

he had once carried me as his impermanent bride,

his emotional orphan, upstairs to our wedding breakfast.

I still drink the same tea each morning as I did back

then though everything else has changed. The currency of

my 'now without him' days is a constant, foreign threshold.

Putney was an affluent suburb, it was sorely unfit for

beginners like us, but the owner (afeard of squatters)

let us rent her mansion for cheap, conspiring against

paying more taxes to an Empire she loved/hated/loved.

She was a famous writer, she was from the colonies, she was

kind, and forgetting her and those times is a cruel capsizing.

The Castle. The Highwayman. The Rose and Crown. The Earl

Spencer. The Robin Hood. The Eight Bells. The Quill.

Always, the quill.

Everybody has forgotten Berlin

I didn't think it was a big deal, going

alone to East Berlin to see some theatre,

but got forlorn on the UBahn. The ghost

stations were argon to my mouth, and

I emerged in Alexanderplatz as aftermath.

My husband was in Mitte drinking with friends,

I was tired of them and their arguments

and rants against conscription, and their

heroic bullshit of 'Here in Berlin I am free', as

though everybody were a jam donut at a disco.

What were any of them doing other than

curating nonsense plans? But here, in the East!

On stage was a Marxist miracle of dedication:

what a pity we are all such whores for the future.

PS *Shade, dass sie eine Hure ist | Tis Pity She's A Whore*, was

the name of the play, and also the story of my long-lost life.

Putney Bridge, Wednesday evening

From the middle of the bridge in the suburb of my marriage
I stopped walking to gaze at her: London. Nothing beats her,
but—up above was the Concorde on her way to New York.
Below me, the brawny Thames wanted to know, *What better,
more beautiful secrets could the Hudson possibly hold?* I was
meant to be working the snow season in Vale, and maybe I'm
married because I was refused that American Visa, and my
teaching life is hard, it's really hard, but for now, the fine
fretwork of London Town is all. *Ohhh*, she is so supersonic, the
Concorde, she'll be there in three-and-a-half hours! Is New
York better than this, Friday nights at the Forum, Saturdays in
Notting Hill, Sundays on the Heath, my whole life a library?
I blow the Concorde a livermorium kiss, but pack no bags, for
upstream in Chelsea is a hospital where one day soon

                                        I will be cut open with child.

PART 2
Womanhood | Prose Poems

Where our elderly heroine likes to walk around in her pyjamas, muttering things like *This fucking world, in which I've wasted my life on the ecstasy of craving*, as though she were accurately, wittingly quoting Sharon Olds.

You've been married 20 years and watched a lot of TV

Because he is not your first husband. You'd been reading William Blake for most of the day, because that is what you get paid to do. *If you think that's fun*, you say in your sad, smartarse way, *You've obviously never read William Blake all day*. But I bet I've done your job, and know your pain, you think, though you guess that's the kind of rude thing a citizen of the creative class says to their rich, professional friends because you are indeed as rude as they are rich. You are sometimes nice to your husband. That evening you continue your television obsession of late, (you are too poor to attend the theatre), viewing the scandalous dead, which is like eating your own teeth. Consider John Profumo, the British Government Minister, Secretary for War (there's a clue) caught having a dirty affair with the young and beautiful and reckless goodtime girl Christine Keeler, she of the famous I-can-spread-my nakedness-all-over-your-wooden-chair fame. It was 1963, the year of your birth. Too much fun was had by Profumo's girls in a London Mews, a stylish, bohemian, risqué abode that once housed unwild horses, but now hosted Russian spies (who did not come for the architectural experience). The sex was spectacular. Afterwards, Profumo said he was sorry to his wife, and she said *I hope she was worth it*, and he answered, without taking his tie off, *Some unspeakable things happened to me in the war*, then devoted the rest of his life to charity work. Is anything forgivable about the 20th century? After serving on the Russian front, for example, is it really OK to sleep with your wife's mother on a bad day? Wait: that wasn't Profumo, that was your father-in-law. Hells on earth clearly all have a sexual accountancy, ask Christine. Profumo is a good name for a perfume, better than Penance, or Prostitute. Poor Christine is dead now. She was a teenage model in 1960s London, a nightclub hostess, a white girl kissing black boys in Notting Hill before Notting Hill kissed Hollywood. She was the packet mix for desire, just add vodka. *I was just doing what we all did*, said all men to all wives, once caught inside Christine's cake box. *I was just having some fun, Mum*, said Christine to her mother, although Holloway Prison was not so funny. When Christine was older and rode her bike all over London, she said she'd been groomed, curated by Steven Ward, osteopath to the Aristocracy, mews man extraordinaire. He seemed like a good friend to you, you wish he'd been your friend, even Blake might have mistaken him for a patron and made an etching of him, or on him. Blake, in another century, a less sexy one, lived just south of the river from Steven's Marylebone mews home, in Lambeth, and once saw an angel stand in the sun upon the bleached wooden floors of his study. It is peculiar whom you invite into your home, and the damage that is done. Christine thought she was an angel. With your first husband, who called you *cherub*, you didn't watch so much TV. You lived a strange, bass (sometimes baritone) life of harpsichord errors that you were too uneducated to register. Instead, in your London home, he read to you in bed, in Italian, or in German, from his favourite writers. This made you fluent in nothing but sleep, and you had to wait for another husband to deliver you things angelic. Yet lately you have forgotten, and instead beg the television to convey them to you afresh. You say to the television, *I swear I've sold myself enough to buy my mother a house with my earnings too*, but the television just ignores you. *Look at me*, you say. The TV says no. A child has awoken from sleep, you are terribly needed, this will be written on your tombstone.

You remember East Germany

Because you are kids. You are kids, and reason has dropped out of you, and you have dropped out of it. But the snow makes everything gentle, with its hush and glamour, its wet, sparkly trippiness like a cosmic rockpool, and in this silence you grow up. Here in Leipzig, the Christmas markets are hopeful, like East Germany once was, before the Wall and its fall. *Wir wollen raus*, the citizens claimed, wanting out. You do not want out, you are happy here, looking around for your husband's stern sister who is posing as the new Director of the Antiquities Museum, perhaps she even is. You are visiting her from Berlin, she is lonely for her husband and his hometown Munich (whose Christkindlmarkt will eat you alive). More snow. Handcrafted leather-goods. Wooden toys. Your sister-in-law buys decorations to adorn her tree, in years to come they will choke her with their beauty and spiked memories, long after she has surrendered to God, because *wir wollen raus*—we always want out. Germany is fully reunited and boss, again, of everything, even her. Decembers in Sydney are kinder than here, despite their savage sand and raw froth and stripped, crazy-blue skies. Here in Leipzig, kiss after kiss, the snow has something to tell your upturned face, and you are listening because last October outside Saint Nicholas Kirche you had been in a crowd that held candles in one hand, and cupped flames with the other, so that no-one had free hands left to hold guns. *Wir sind das Volk*, we are the people. It is all over now. The people without guns, we won. The hospitals threw away their extra stocks of blood transfusions. Tonight, alone together, you go out to a disco, the Westerners storming the bar, the Easterners queueing politely, deeply expressionless, faithful for what is to come. On the dance floor they are orderly, tightly slim, momentarily wild dancers, uninterested in stories about Sydney or sin. There is after all nothing about decadence that wasn't already Russian. You sit in a corner and talk softly with a soldier about geology, about how some rockpools fill with sea anemones, and others, portentous bones, like parapets, and he told you about his traitor mother, and the true taste of bananas. The Scorpions owned the dancefloor. The CIA were everywhere. We all wanted out. You did not know then if you were water or ice, fish or line, east or west, nor that you would never be so free again.

Keep your linen press in order

Because you've come home to live, new bikinis in your car boot. Beachside mansions have munched the weatherboard shacks, your girlhood home shirks in their pale shadows. The truth-telling moon rises. Next morning, the king tide has shaven the white history of the beach away, layer by layer, and there it is: the black-grained blood beneath, the stained, forensic evidence of sandmining. You want to know who got rich off that travesty, and marry their finest offspring. Afterwards you will both drink too much, every day, from 5pm onwards, and pine for the past, and strive to make amends, to be better than your robber-baron parents. But you are so drunk you will spill champagne on the cheque book, making your signatures as blurred and useless as your good intentions. *It is not my land*, you will say, lit up by the sunset. *The elders don't own country, country owns itself* (you've raised your voice) *but why had she just lain there like a whore and let us take her?* Oh dear. You are so very in-vino-veritas smashed. Reconciliation is your hobby, your play-dough paste, with it you try to glue yourself back together. You are so cracked and antique someone should put you in a pristine period drama about paradise lost, but instead you just keep blathering 'peace' and 'love' and accidentally eat the arsenic-laced picnic damper. You die. You rise again. You get really mad, wondering why that was the best plan you could think of, to marry. You would do anything, it seems, to make amends, even marry your enemy if he was rich enough to pay the past to slouch away. Still drunk one morning, you go down to the beach and decide to sit there until the future arrives, hoping she has a better story. It is bloody cold. Before sunrise, you've gone home and unpacked the dishwasher and packed the lunches and folded the nappies and fully understand despite your throbbing, resistant head that there are centuries of work ahead, but you don't care, you like a good mess to sort out, you were not born into the Protestant cult for nothing.

One night in Sarsaparilla, walking exempt through hell

Because of all the postcodes, this one explains what happens next. The suburb one over (and where is Virgil when you need him?) is full of sunny women, but in Sarsaparilla—since the plague and after the war—the frauen snap like whiplash with divine anger at the simony of their lives. Better and brighter than their employed husbands, they are by law housebound, by disposition dangerous. But Friday nights are glorious—

on Friday nights (for you might as well live) they party, masked, anonymous, un-curfewed, free, until dawn. Tonight, the bash is at Donna's, so watch out wild world, and yeah, Not tonight Satan, and Not tomorrow either Santa. Dominus Domina Donna. But where is Donna? Marianne can't find her anywhere. She's not in the darkling plain of the pantry slumming it with the drunken servants where, swept with confused alarms of struggle and flight and too much vodka, ignorant armies clash by night. 'Give it back, give it me back, give it up you—' and so on, their motto *did not could not but maybe might.* But life is not a Margaret Atwood novel, there are no endearments beneath the bed. The bedrooms? Upstairs she goes, singing—

'Donna Donna Donna?'

On the landing the stairs split like two roads diverging in a wood. 'I secretly long for the apocalypse. Then I could remember what is truly important,' said a naked woman to a suited man. He kindly wrapped her in her discarded robe and replied 'As uncertainty breeds anxiety and ill-being, we witness institutions reacting to protect the fabric of their existence rather than of our being.' They kissed. Marianne took the empty stairs, to the left, less travelled by sadness, and that has made all the difference. Swelling from the living room below: breaking glass, crying, laughing, music, shouting, snatches of conversation—*That was decades ago/Frenzied fists fighting to hoard toilet rolls, emptied shopping aisles/Even lying under a heavy duvet makes me claustrophobic/I have been putting off my dental work, but now I go/I love leaves. They are so reliable. There is, well, there was—this is absolutely true—a country that spoke in the language of leaves/Are they dreaming of escape?/Apples taste better this year, I find. Don't you think?/I have the dog at least.* Eventually, all faded to nonsense. Aside from the business Marianne found in every bedroom (where no time was wasted on love) and the party-drug laboratory in the bathroom (where devotees were being squeezed and dried till blue is black by that terrible dye, thinking of a dawn that might not come), evidence of —

what exactly was she looking for? Outside in the garden by the pool where she washed her eyelids in the rain Marianne began to drink, joining in, trying. But—sorry this isn't more profound I feel like everything is surface at the moment. Our friends become dead announcements at the same desk where we stream our hope There is no ergonomic set-up that softens the silence of a bully. Something's happening in Laos. The Rosedale eggs didn't break if you dropped them on the floor—little made sense. She forgot to pray for the angels and held onto herself like a crucifix. The party was unfolding on the edge of itself. Shortly after 9pm—

Donna found her. They vowed to say yes to everything. In the kitchen, Marianne took off her bra, and kissed everyone in the room. She could feel her legs growing again. Her legs! All the better to strangle you with. Donna's friend from Suburb Seven arrived, and talked too much. She was a bad smell, a bad bet, a bad joke, she was. Her breasts were enormous, planets demoted to dwarfs. The evening soured, knowing they were all, anyway, on a wagon bound for market. She was drunk, and bored with having legs, praying now for the return of her thick, shocking, private, fishy, mermaid tail. She wanted everything back. The whole evening had become—

too much, too mournful eyed, too wallflower-at-the-disco. With the chef's knife last used for necking champagne bottles, Marianne began to make delicate cuts on her arm. Just beneath her skin one gash revealed a howling baby, another a nest of gold coins, yet another (deeper now) five soiled petticoats. Cut cut cut—look! There is peace, how pretty it is!—until the opera reached its certain conclusion, the knife heading towards gooseflesh for the final act. We know how this party ends: this poem is an appetite. Dominus Domina Donna, mea domina.

The Great Ocean Road, January last

Because at Lorne, police were policing the dawn road alive with ocean dew and blood. There is no way through for you. A bus, a car full of teenage girls, the wrong kind of hit and kiss, no way out for them but up to the crying sky. The rescue helicopters carry the almost-dead and their witnesses angel-fast back to Royal Melbourne Hospital. Who's saving who here, you wonder, turning inland as instructed, the only route left opened. Country towns zoom in on you with their soft focus. You are not crying, they are not your children, you don't know anyone here, you have enough petrol in your tank to drive past all roadkill perhaps to Mumbai, you're just waiting for the highway to build itself. Over your shoulder (left) the ocean begs for your return and (right) crazed survivors from a bush doof stumble from the stringybarks. You were tempted to buy a tractor at Colac, you were tempted to buy wine at Tilly's vineyard, and muffins in the village of women wearing peasant dresses, but the act of purchase had lost its tranquilizing effect. The girls from the accident were dead. It was being broadcast already. You were road-tripping with your daughter the sunflower, and this time you had no surfboards or dogs and those girls of the accident of the early morn were even longer dead by the time you looped back to the thin coastal road and reached the Southern Ocean Villas at Port Campbell where you always stayed but of which your daughter had no recall. But you have proof. You have a photo of you all taken by the nanny, it is a picture of a father and a mother and five children attached to your limbs like mutations, behind you is water fresh from cold Antarctica with much to moan about, and the famous rocks they call the Apostles who likewise vibrate with news. But you are even deafer now than you were then and have nothing worthy to pass on. You are still frightened of the long-gone nanny. Here we are, there we were, on the crusty-lipped edge of the country with roads centimeters away from water, sinking towards the final pole. It is not relaxed, it is not an English meadow, this unreconciled landscape of home. What did you expect but a soap opera with sirens? You'd expected better from the weekend, from this beautiful, impossible road built by hopeful people. Swap those adjectives and you have the real truth: there's a holiday snap for you.

Resignation letter written by wolf-light

Because she wrote, *Dear Sue, Hope you're well. This is to let you know your application for teaching relief has been denied. By the way, I have cautioned the Dean against allowing you any further leadership roles considering how sick your children are. The stress you are under has made you unreliable—your students are complaining, your colleagues have had enough. It would be beneficial I'm sure for you to have some time off. I therefore strongly recommend reducing your employment to part-time, given your personal circumstances. PS Please take care.* Because, we all get versions of emails like this. Because, weaponised wellbeing missives from colleagues are not kind, not from people who think you aren't actually teaching hundreds of online students, but instead sucking your own cock. Because, last year you won the university's highest award, but must have been mistaken. Because you've published so many books, it must be time for you to perish. Because 'We've all had COVID'—and your accompanying heart attack must have been imaginary. Because 'You are an obstructive bitch, I don't have to show you fucking evidence!' texts from your colleagues who refuse to table proof of the invisible complaints made about your teaching are killing you. Because you don't drink with them, because they are fuckwits. Because you read this email in Accident & Emergency, praying, yet again, for your child's life. She's on life support. You silently pass your phone, show the email, to the Psychiatric Registrar when she asks *How are you?* She reads it while you kiss your unconscious, rare-diseased, autistic, anorexic, addicted, suicidal child's head, the smell of the streets on her like dystopia's arrival. The psych gives you back your phone, it is radioactive now. The heart monitor crawls into your mouth, submarine bleeping. This is how you are, you are turning posthuman. You both laugh at the monstrous message, it's absurd cruelty, you laugh like brittle, thirsty rice bubbles, because you needed some light relief and what really matters is always, anyway, a funny business at 3am in an inner-city hospital with linoleum floors looking up your skirt, their gleam striking your chin, threatening to snatch your daughter, swallow her alive. You can hear missiles. You're breaking some legal code of conduct, sharing that university email, that's for sure. But not the moral code of saying no to unkindness, to discrimination. Of saying no to the oppression of depression, the poison within the boil of workplace bullying. Something is being launched. You can feel yourself inflating, becoming huger, your blue skin stretching over the entire hospital like a Christo installation. *Sue me if you don't like the show*, you think. And, *Beware us post-twilight women*, you also think, thanking the psych, watching the monitors, holding your daughter's undead hand. *You'd better beware.*

The hour between dog and wolf is no more.

Furyology

Because as a stepmother—what with the simony of love the position demands—you are a disappointment. Their cuddles were barbed with pity, they raised their eyes from their cots expecting their true mother, and it was just you, so it was all minor-crime this and imagined-sleight that from then on, but you were too stupid not to be nice. Besides, in the poppling days of your beginnings, when love arched over you like a wintergaw, there was a chance to succeed at this business of secondhood. Their rightful mother, her spirit pickled in swill, kept firing canons from the Firth of Forth to your new home in Stockbridge. Direct hits, always. Large promises, scant fulfilments, this was your experience of the local supermarket, and of second marriages in general. Your trunk was soon split with the ex-wife's lightning, your hope thundered dead. You left the roarie bummler of the blended family to the Scots and went back to London, far from the fast-moving storm clouds of the north, all the way home to Hackney. Hackney with its knives and tribes and cheap recording studios and print-moonlight skies on summer nights, the reliable winter-proud of the River Lea, the café teas strong enough to fuel fighter engines. He came to you eventually, your husband, without his girls, he came with all his grief afire, came to warm you and only you, and the thawing cost you both forever. They are grown now, those girls, but also not. You are still changing their nappies, and dumbly waiting for the thanks that will never arrive, because babies are babies and you are just a silly woman in love with the wrong man—theirs.

I still love you (the damage is done)

1

Because the bus nearly fell over at the corner of Barbara Hepworth's house in St Ives. It was going too fast but the real problem was the weight of the passengers, their heavy judgements, tipping the beast, *She left her children you know, hard to admire a woman like that.* At the Tate Gallery you touched one of her sculptures, *Talk to me you bitch*, you hoarsely whispered, then went out onto the sunshine-licked patio above the crackling sea and watched the dolphins who could not care less about women and their freedoms and their 20th century tantrums. What a postcard life can be. Later, back in London, you tried to discuss this with your husband but the cat was biting to be fed, the dog pawing to be walked, the children needing to be driven to work and to score drugs, so you kept your existential mutterings to yourself. Still, stacking the dishwasher, you wonder if you had such fine intelligence within you, to walk around the trap, to deposit your children as fresh foundlings beneath Peter Pan's statue in Kensington Gardens and run. You have so much freedom it is killing you, you breathe the bad breath of its lullaby, you stay and inhale. You miss Cornwall like home. You miss the lonely sea, who sometimes groans like a woman, moving the boulders beneath, cresting then crashing. The lights of Hackney laugh.

2

Because it is late at night in Melbourne, you're reading yourself to sleep, and you can hear the love calls of the powerful owls, their noisy kick-off to the mating season making your womb itch. They are about to go possum shopping in their urban bush, you are about to carry your own body weight of grief to the night for its rinsing. You've read all her books, have always read all her books, but the biography grates your cortex, pierces your kidneys. Doris Lessing endured sex as small ceremonies of hatred, then she turned 50 and instantly and suddenly and deliberately jumped ship from womanhood, surrendered overnight to uncrossed legs with varicose veins like pipelines gassing Jupiter, and a severe hairstyle, a dead-squirrel kind of bun. Giver-upperer on romance, how dare she, she who had flung her children to Africa for devouring so that she might *live live live* but where are all her lovers now? Her books unsettled you. Before you read Lessing you were a locked mind, a furled heart ready to stroke or crack, a citizen scientist awaiting a proper education. That was you, and now all you are is the reading, and the damage done. You decide, as your husband momentarily wakes and kisses your back, that reading Doris Lessing in bed is madness. *Whoo hoo, whoo hoo* ask the owls: yes, you trill, with your trapped tongue, *I still love you.*

I still love you.

Rainy day with a merchant banker

Because the iron gate of the gated gardens thumped shut. Because he had such a psychic weight, my companion, he was so extremely wealthy, he impressed everybody and everything including the proteins within me, even the unborn blades of grass beneath. His wife, your best friend, had had an urgent appointment with her obstetrician, and your husband had gone to Leicester for undeclared business (you were furious as sin at him). So there you both were on that stray Saturday, sheltering from the maybe-rain beneath an unwilling plane tree. It was all so backdoor-Bloomsbury, your babies in pouches, the older kids in the forbidden flower beds behaving like bloody revolutionaries, wooden swords ahigh. This is England, Peter Pan will be here soon. You could smell a cello arching out of a window in Mecklenburgh Square, the pretty square that was once so very bombed and so very loved by the Queen. You were damp, you were cold, it was after all January, *How could you leave all this*, he joked, being well-versed in the destination of your tomorrows, your soon-return to the subtropics whose beaches his smarter-than-me wife had once also escaped. His dreams needed the City, they included making even more money than Cleopatra could swallow, and financing his own film company, for fun. His wife speaks Japanese and Mandarin and French and Swahili and is sexily absent-minded at every dinner party of theirs you've ever attended. You will miss her smile and her stiff anarchy and her sisterly scolding and her cast-off clothes. Their five children will grow into a new breed of unicorn; your five will famously reinvent seaside serfdom. Whatever. It's all over now. It tasted like bush honey that cello music, straining your heart with longing, the notes sliding in and out and around the soft raindrops, who were really spies, intent on my demise. Honey with a high note of eucalypt. Or cobalt? You'd once married a motorbike, so you deserved everything metallic to come.

After the collapse (pregnant again)

Because when you opened your eyes, first off you saw the kitchen door, weary from wearing everybody's touch. You were on the floor, which you'd just cleaned and still smelt of lavender, but was now blistered with vomit. You felt a soft wetness on the side of your head, saw blood on your fingers and the edge of the chair. Tried to get up, failed. The pain was bad, as though you were turning from girl into woman into myth, discarding your bones. You blacked out, blued in, peaceful with this sampler of death. You had not once thought of your mother. So this is freedom, you thought, watching the sunlight's tidal rushing against the stained glass of the windows, its whirling amongst the wooden cabinetry, the white chairs looking like shy, dutiful children, blessed. You regarded those chairs with an abounding love, such as you had never felt before. Arising, ghostly, you splashed your face above the sink, the water echoing like a tin dinghy on the sea. Your beautiful, rockpool of a sink, with its hightide, lowtide life: You love your sink. *Dear God, protect me.* In the window you met your stranger-face. They will be home from school soon, back from business shortly, there is no need for them to see you fainting with pregnancy. The supper was unprepared, the first aid kit was nowhere to be seen, the baby was awake and crying. What an experiment the rest of your life has become.

The decisions of women

1 Psychology is a science but it does not explain today

Because four a.m. does not exist but three a.m. does. Three a.m. is the blunt lead of night, it sinks your boat, and come morning you crawl ashore from the dark haemorrhage into the day, whose sunshine is about to have its way with you. This is the tiredness of women. You are not who you began as. Even though you have too much education and a full peg basket, a bright plastic rainbow of pulled teeth, and have broken your fast with homemade muesli so healthy that it would choke the engine of a tank, you think: today might be the day you fail. It is no one's fault but yours. You have chosen everything. You have laid down for love. So you carry on, you kiss and smile and pack swimming bags and white wash and hills hoist and come lunchtime do drugs for their evasive quietude and detumescence. But you can't fool everyone with your 1970s style inattention, your upcycled fascism, daydreaming a miscarriage to bury beneath the jasmine. You are pregnant. You must choose. Please try not to be symbolic.

2 Letter to your child, about to die

Because it is perfect. This glad morning on the day of death, you lay in bed and hold the child in your womb, dancing to the bounce of kitten sunlight shifting across your belly. And what a beautiful day it is. Before you diarise it, after the abortion, you tell your unborn child everything it would ever need to know: in the world war to come before it kills you, the cats will side with America, the oceans will leave for Mars, the love of fathers will continue to burn, the forests will eat themselves, dancing is forbidden, poets become politicians, and love has been genetically bred out, so why not end it now? You ask your child, *Perhaps you grasp all this already?* The deeds of mothers are (contrary to global marketing) rarely kind these days, capitalism has made you more complex and destructive, smitten by exhaustion. Mistakes like mushrooms flourish within the fields of women. But *I am not imprudent*, you say to your child, *I am undefeated, my taboo business of the day is one of excessive love. The surgical kiss coming your way soon is of the heaven-sent kind, all gods that save are built of sanitised steel.* Then you stop with the talking. You have an urgent appointment. You have promised your child the utmost: that no more pain than this will be theirs.

The niece goes batshit then declares it a draw

Because you knew him before he went to Vietnam to fight. Most people blame his death on his failed love affair with the bouncy, bored wife from the tennis club, but you'd long seen the ruin in his eyes. Sometimes at Christmas or weddings some relative as drunk as an undergraduate would recall your Uncle's cinematic nightmares, his campsite screams swallowed by the gumtrees, suffered by all. He loved lots of women, you can remember them all, from the barmaid to the barrister's wife, because their fashion choices fastened themselves to you like fishhooks, you swallowed the bait of womanhood they merchandised. Your dress-up box is now full of very short frocks made of moonshine, crocheted bikinis lined with arsenic, love beads strung on guts, and Valium-inspired velour sportswear—anything really from that false era of granola freedom. Your Aunty took it bad, she ate the suicide notes left for your cousins, his children, and his lies lived inside her like bad tapeworms. She took the hose from the car's exhaust and put it back to work sprinkling the garden, returned the unfinished carton of beer from the boot to the bottleshop, threw it through their window, and slept with the empty cans he'd drunk, squashed like failed horseshoes, beneath her pillow. You were not invited to the funeral but you went anyway, you wore his favourite dress once slashed now made of cellophane and silk. You still have the records you stole at his wake although you never play them for fear of raising the helicopters, inciting national conscription, electrifying the velocity between then and now. Old now, you hide this uranium store from your own children because such misfortune demands a saga to tell and you never will. You inherit his house; no one ever talks to you again. He owed you much, this is not enough, but what did you expect, Sappho's lost poems, the Florentine diamond, the Nazi gold from Lake Toblitz, one stolen treasure as compensation for another? He meant to hurt you with his dying, but you had more fun burning his house down than he ever did with napalm.

You can't really count the ways

Because lately he has taken up running. For his age he is about as handsome as they come, whereas plastic surgery was invented for the way you look. After sixteen years of locked-down life—or six months, you no longer know—after this long, long time you are not the same. Things have been stolen from you by that indiscriminate thief of experience who swagged the whole house one drunken night. Come the morning the foretold future was gone, all schooling was forsaken, someone had been locked in a hospital like a contagious mistake, the washing had sewed itself into Rapunzel's solution, and the animals had learnt to drive, stolen the cars, fled for the border. In the left-behindedness there was just the two of you, as though that had always been your only intention, the in-fact purpose of your first kiss, the paradise that is the island of husband and wife after the heavy seas. Is that your husband on the shoreline, far ahead of you, still running from the shipwreck of you? Go ahead, you think. While he is gone you will beachcomb the bejesus out of the debris, build a new home, and like a locked compass wait for his return, your love: because islands are only ever reliably round.

Hotel sex before and after it was invented

1

Because in other galaxies love has been bred out, heartbreak does not exist, divorce is unwarranted. So now, hotels are ancient monuments of tourism, statues in the holocaust-garden of planet earth. Dangerous and forbidden shrines, for VIP visitors only, they sit empty and glorious, dead giants, brimful of the singing souls they once consumed, archaeology of the last operas on earth. But before the future, on this last chance getaway, in this still-alive world, your man recalls that you are his pretty mistress, his museum piece, and he is your curator. Hope catalogues within you, that he might change his mind, purchase you for his private collection.

2

Because it wasn't only you who spread the rot of durian around. On your first-ever night in America you kissed the hotel janitor to thank him for fixing the air-conditioning and because you liked his cowboy eyes. Even though he'd left the door ajar in some kind of good-faith gesture, the room was soon all mouth and tongue and hips and hands. You came together in soundbites of suicide. 'Holy Cow,' you thought, and other phrases fresh from *Happy Days*, that land of milkshakes and leather jackets. He needed to visit a decent dentist, your room service man, he needed to stop saying, 'Give me everything you've got, you fat, white bitch'. But Hollywood is not Beverly Hills: fact to know. The next day you concluded your business with LA, and left, your vagina a dull register of everything you'd purchased, or been given for free.

3

Because this happened. There are three-hundred-and-thirty-two inhabited volcanic islands off of Fiji and you stayed on one of them with your husband one December to avoid a family Christmas. You'd been married for more than a decade and were unprepared for the honeymoon slap of the resort, full of fresh couples kissing like baby seagulls. You went snorkelling every day and once swam through a battery of barracuda. You turned yourself into a silver flying fish, you built a church, you ate sand, you grew thinner than oxygen, and laid down each night for your husband like the end was slouching in the shower. On Christmas eve the islanders went from bure to bure serenading the guests with carols. It was holy and cruel. You thought, what am I doing here? Shouldn't the beach, that most murderous site of dispossession, after all, be a reminder to be better? A memorial to slaughter, prose for reconciliation? As weak and stupid as autumn, you let everything drop. Then, suddenly, the sunshine that once hid everything from you splits you open. You start speaking to each other again. You allow him his violent sovereignty of you. By the time you get home to Sydney you are both happy graduates of horror.

4

Because here you are now, with your hard usage of yourself hiding beneath the bed in your clifftop hotel in Tathra (soon to be burnt out by a bushfire). You are trying again to recall love (why is he hitting me?) in a rundown joint chosen for its incinerating bewitchment. This is your last anniversary, though you did not then know how soon you would be unwed and dead. You had waited for him dressed like you once spied your mother — brunette, salon-styled hair, red lips like plastic knuckles, black petticoat, straps astray, drinking whiskey straight up from the toothbrush glass, playing solitaire. The woman on the bed makes the mirror warp and arch, she is so beautiful. It is really you. The man is a lesson you need, and need again, you are so foolish. This is fake news, you are not that woman, you were never there. Tomorrow, you will again become all that is unbegun.

A short history of thin

Because heading for the hospital to visit your girl you listen to an audiobook about a mother's story of caring for her anorexic daughter. Because you need advice like the dead need dirt. She didn't seem to do a very good job, that mother, because her girl died. Hearing her story makes you grow so large you have to turn sideways to fit through the tram doors to exit at your stop. You are so huge walking up to the psychiatric ward your feet burst from your shoes, and you are the only person allowed to ride the lift, but by the time you pass ward security you are thin again, thinner than a traduced memory. You remember, for example, your Aunty eating Limits Diet Biscuits for years and years, you used to steal the chocolate ones, she slapped your wrists, first one and then the other, wordlessly, steam coming out her nose. You don't blame her, they were expensive food items and hard to get in country towns: they came with free gossip. Oprah went to Rome for a holiday, treated herself to cheesy pasta, then ran round and round the Colosseum the next morning, as instructed by her fitness instructor. Liz Hurley eats cabbage soup for ten days before each Caribbean holiday because it is bad manners to be a bore on a diet at society gatherings. Your dieting Aunty got cancer after her husband suicided. He was a Vietnam veteran, more Australian soldiers have died like this since than during the war. He had to eat tinned eggs during active service, who wouldn't kill themselves? Their marriage had been a strange shopping list for a supermarket that did not exist. Before she died your Aunty jerked upright and vomited, hugely, splendidly, enough to fill the Trevi Fountain. When she'd holidayed in Rome her thin bottom was never pinched, though her fat daughter barely got out of the place alive. When you get out of this hospital, you're taking your daughter to Rome and never coming home, you have found the clinic you need, the clinic is called pizza. You are going to make a plan, a good plan, but no one can make a good plan in a locked psychiatric ward, so you make a note to yourself to make a good plan as soon as you escape from this visit. This visit involves a frightening conversation about medication which saws off your arms from the shoulders. Then you have a conversation about the excellent range of vegan food available in Coles supermarkets. Apparently. So the inmates have said. You are bleeding all over the place, will no one help? All you know is which supermarket has the best Weight

Watchers ready meals in stock because you are a fool of many inheritances. An utter fool in need of being wrapped up. You slap your own thin-lady wrists with your amputated arms, then hold her close, your vanishing love child, in your inadequate way, because clearly this is all your fault, including the fact that you are now armless. You talk about missing the ocean. You talk about who is in trouble for what violations on the ward. One of the male nurses accidentally hooked up with the Psychiatric registrar on Grinder (who—it's now official—is a useless fuck). Hilarious. Your daughter has to leave now, to eat a disgusting sandwich made by someone who never loved her, never will. When you get home you will drink alcohol, you will fuck that wine like you are gladly enslaved, because you can never write about this, and someone has to consume the calories that life commands, before a new century arrives that loves women better the last.

Set free

Because you worry about what to wear. You worry if the stingrays beneath you will kill you. On Mondays you worry about wasted weekends and on Fridays you fret over squandered weeks. There is the worry of whether he ever loved you, the worry of what you did to your children and if you'll ever know, the worry of warts, the worry of drinking too much, the worry of age-appropriate fashion and hairstyles, the worry of the vast claims of the past, the worry of a poorly-lived life, all the worries of a narcissistic wife, the worry of wondering if you'll ever learn anything about anything let alone this, the worry of recovery from major surgery, the worry of losing friends, the worry of answering or not answering unknown callers, the worry of debt, the worry of drought, the worry of bushfires, the worry of planning anything let alone everything, the worry of too-high heels, the worry of democracy, the worry of error, the worry of the last kiss and if you'll ever know, the worry of your wishes, the worry of suicide being more intoxicating than Christmas and your having forsaken all that is Santa Claus, the worry of anorexia and her queen-bee autocracy, the worry of not knowing, and again, the worry of what to wear in all the seasons of worry, the worry of the worry before it grew to dread. All this you worry about, waiting, being handled by the staff as un-alarmedly as a thornless rose, for your daughter to be discharged from her nine-week stay. That's about how long it takes for a kangaroo to gestate, or a fox: You are terribly busy worrying about what the psych ward has rebirthed her as this time, and what kind of mother you must now rapidly become.

You hack yourself

Because, overnight, the Eating Disorder Unit in the city's best hospital became a locked psychiatric ward due to one young woman (after brushing her hair) trying to eat herself. Because her belief was: I am nothing; I will have no effect on myself; I do not matter; I have no matter; my consumption is of no account. The next day, no weight was gained by anyone, human or posthuman, anywhere in the entire world. When cats groom, this is in preparation for outer space, hoping for bulimic expectoration of furballs ahead of takeoff, for who knows about the truth of gravity or the value of what we swallow and regurgitate? Or indeed any unseen chamber of concealed, ambitious mess? Princess Diana had a very sad relationship to food before her marriage, and during, but not afterwards. Because afterwards her pirouetting galaxy became cake-built and guilt-free, with castles prince-full of nice young men who just wanted to dance. Tonight our patient begins her evening in the ballroom with the princess, then she trips, then pounces, turning feral, then arches back into a patient, then a person, then a pumpkin. In the hospital kitchen they throw away her ballet pumps and bake her into a pumpkin pie. The pie is served as a midnight feast, a prescription for the others girls, with a label that reads 'Eat Me, Eat Me Not'. Because girls are always in some kind of love, and need their sustenance, and would kill themselves before hurting a cat.

Glorious micrographica

Because at the petrol station the stranger smiled at you, winked, drove away. Beautifully shocked, you suddenly felt all lipstick-and-limbs, heading home from the hospital through the petticoated suburbs. Married so long that even your wedding ring was worn out, you determined to be cheerier, beginning with a sexy supper, remote as possible from motherly purpose. Inside your fridge there remains a meagre confetti of leftover ingredients: some good cheese; crisp green apples; an unused passport; a broken, wooden ruler; three bold tomatoes; a shelf of anguish that smelt of off oyster; one stray, frozen, thawing limb; six unopened bottles of pale Italian wine with absurdly thin necks; and a tin box sealed with blue wax. Vertigo seizes you, subsides. What should you wear? A dragonfly collides with the window above the sink. Or was it Tinkerbell? You think of Icarus falling into the sea with his imposter wings asunder, the sun-melted wax burning his skin: failure at the hands of hubris, they say, but really, you blame his foolish father. Ask any mother about escaping any labyrinth and she'll come up with a better plan than

Daedalus and his dodgy inventions, his worthless warnings. Your life is drowned, you suddenly realize, no longer the phosphorescent wonder it once was before this plague began, and death became your daughter's third lung. The hospitals are failing. One of them has eaten your daughter, you are convinced. The churches are closed. Condoms remain unwrapped. Children know too much about syringes. Curfews at dusk choke the bad-mannered city whose citizens shout at dogs for being happy. Crows have never been your friends. All this is true. Yet—this afternoon you had been brazenly admired. You seize this jewel, which belongs to you anyway, grip it in your hand like a lost tooth. You pack your strange picnic, and head for the highway.

Today is Friday (says the relief teacher, offering relief)

Because, minding your own business, waiting for them to finish their exam, you notice your pencil is 'Made in Germany', and the school motto on its shaft translates to 'hard work and faith'. A graduate of this school was murdered not so long ago. Would she want her name carved in memorial stone, upgraded into Latin, made motto? Over lunch, you're on playground duty and pace the fields where she spent her last minutes, her final, fearful seconds. You have to break up a lover's tiff, and get one kid to return another's phone. You're umpiring for an invisible empire of lost love. Too old for this, you are, and hungry, and those sweet children who've taken a liking to you just make you think of your own insolvency as a mother. Over there by Carlton Football Club you can see the football goal posts, recently choked in flowers, the site of vigils. It had been her only business, that poor, dead girl's, to be gloriously young, not to be buried at 19 just for being too fabulously alive one Friday night, walking alone, almost home. Fiasco that you are, next lesson you're teaching Revolutions. Because.

One day soon your son will ask if you were ever a groupie

Because you knew so much too young, and the joy of this lived inside your teeth like aluminium, and your smile was a flipped Sydney Harbour Bridge. Because you loved to dance, because the night. The things you did not know begun with how to unkiss someone, or cook capsicum with conviction, and included how to go to class sober, or imagine the adult future, how to spell superannuation, or live within the cobweb feel of a mortgaged home, or the helter-skelter of the years to come with their graduations and rings and holidays and haircuts and reprimands and emergencies that will render you spineless, until you grow fresh bone that finally stands you upright.

Because once upon a time you loved him. He was your mainland.

Because he skipped soundcheck and went with you to the surgery and sat holding your hand while the doctor contemptuously pushed the abortionist's phone number across the desk. Then this: you refused his love, his pleas of 'this-could-be-so-cool-we-could-take-the-kid-on-the-road-with-us' nonsense. You refused his promises. The terror turned your eyeballs to splinters. You did not refuse the taxi that next weekday morning, or anything that happened next at the Balmain Clinic. You even ate the sandwiches afterwards, drank the tea gleefully, and three years later you did not refuse to laugh when your girlfriend shared her abortion story, and you realised that the both of you—housemates of bandmates back then—had, unbeknownst, been there conducting your killing business on the exact same morning. Precisely. No, you did not refuse to laugh about that absurdity, those two women, rock widows alone (their men on tour), bleeding. Just bloody bleeding.

Because you will laugh till you cry about this forever.

Bonfire night

Because bushfire season is no time for lighting matches or stoking bonfires to burn letters, but you are separated from all regard. At school you knew a boy who lit bushfires, one of his letters is in the bucket ready to glow, *oh*, how you once loved him—but only while he loved another. They always love another. The wallpapered, lifelong repetition of this error, the sticky shock of it, glues you to the fence. You rip apart. You are ready now to transfer to ash the shame in your humiliated heart. You stack the wood by the swimming pool, you call on God. Fire is fire and there she goes, that tractor petrol is vicious, licking the diaries and letters and photos like the devil. Lovers you thought anyway dead are now truly ash, friends who forget your birthday charred, children untutored in love now released from all schooling, your own mother and father, goodly gone, your famous friends, smokily forsaken. Only the fumes can namedrop now. The burning fragments of archival confetti fall from above full of injury, they're not done with you even now. The black night blazes on, streaked blue by your leaving, startled stars making way. This is all that memory wants, this hot forgetting. The future presses down on you like a good husband but you, you happy

woman, you girl set free from history,

        you have sold out to the sky.

ABOUT THE AUTHOR

Susan Bradley Smith is an Australian poet and historian. She grew up in Bundjalung country in rural New South Wales before attending university in Sydney, then working as journalist living in England, Scotland and Germany. Based in Melbourne, she has a doctorate in English Literature, and works as an academic, teacher, and librettist. An award-winning writer, recent books include the memoir *Friday Forever*; the poetry collection *Gladland*; and *A Splendid Adventure*, a critical history of suffragette theatre. *Bonfire Got Hot* is her 10th book, and you can follow her experimental poetry on instagram @bluepoetess.